KT-222-619

Adele
the Singing Coach
Fairy

Special thanks to
Narinder Dhami

ORCHARD BOOKS
338 Euston Road, London NW1 3BH
Orchard Books Australia
Level 17/207 Kent Street, Sydney, NSW 2000
A Paperback Original

First published in 2012 by Orchard Books

© 2012 Rainbow Magic Limited.
A HIT Entertainment company. Rainbow Magic
is a trademark of Rainbow Magic Limited.
Reg. U.S. Pat. & Tm. Off. And other countries.

Illustrations © Orchard Books 2012

A CIP catalogue record for this book is available
from the British Library.

ISBN 978 1 40831 590 3

5 7 9 10 8 6

Printed in Great Britain

The paper and board used in this paperback are natural recyclable
products made from wood grown in sustainable forests. The
manufacturing processes conform to the environmental regulations
of the country of origin.

Orchard Books is a division of Hachette Children's Books,
an Hachette UK company

www.hachette.co.uk

Adele
the Singing Coach Fairy

by Daisy Meadows

ORCHARD

www.rainbowmagic.co.uk

Jack Frost's Ice Castle

Camping Site

Girls' tent

Main Stage

Karaoke tent

Cafe

The Harbour

Rainspell Island

Jack Frost's Spell

It's high time for the world to see
The legend I was born to be.
The prince of pop, a dazzling star
My fans will flock from near and far.

But pop star fame is hard to get
Unless I help myself, I bet.
I need a plan, a cunning trick
To make my stage act super-slick.

Seven magic clefs I'll steal
They'll give me pop star powers, I feel.
I'll sing and dance, I'll dazzle and shine
And pop star glory will be mine!

Contents

A Picnic
Surprise

"What a fantastic place for a picnic!"
Rachel Walker exclaimed, her face
breaking into a huge smile.

She and her best friend, Kirsty Tate,
were standing on a grassy hill above
the site where the Rainspell Island
Music Festival was taking place over five
fun-packed days. Below them the girls
could see the enormous stage surrounded
by lighting rigs and sound equipment.

Close by was Star Village, where festival-goers were able to have a go at being a pop star themselves. The village had a karaoke tent as well as a marquee for dance classes, and there were other areas where people could try out pop star hairstyles and make-up, as well as designing their own stage costumes. There were stalls and food tents, too, and a campsite for festival-goers where Rachel, Kirsty and Rachel's parents were staying.

"OK, girls," called a voice behind them. "The picnic's ready!"

Rachel and Kirsty spun around eagerly. Their friends Serena, Lexy and Emilia, otherwise known as the famous pop group The Angels, were sitting on a fluffy pink picnic rug, smiling up at them. Rachel and Kirsty's eyes grew wide as they saw the three girls surrounded by plates and bowls of delicious food.

"Oh, this looks so glamorous!" Kirsty sighed as she and Rachel joined The Angels on the picnic rug. There were piles of dainty triangular sandwiches scattered with edible glitter, and a crystal glass bowl brimming over with ripe red strawberries alongside another bowl of clotted cream. A jug of freshly made lemonade with floating ice cubes and slices of lemon stood in the cool shade of a nearby tree.

"Well, you two *are* our special festival
guests," Emilia reminded her, passing
Kirsty a china plate piled high with tiny
sandwiches. Kirsty and Rachel had first
got to know The Angels when they'd
won a competition to meet the band,
and since then they'd all
become good friends.

Lexy was
pouring
lemonade
into sparkling
crystal glasses.
"Rainspell Island
is lovely, isn't it?"
she remarked. "So
green and peaceful."

"It's a really magical place,"
Rachel agreed, glancing at Kirsty.

Rainspell Island was where the two girls had first met on holiday – and it was even more special, because it was also where they had discovered that fairies were real! Since then, the girls had shared many thrilling adventures with their tiny, magical friends.

"We have another surprise for you, girls," Serena said when they'd finished eating. She took two books out of the picnic hamper, one bound in pink silk and one in pale blue. The word *Autographs* was embroidered across the front of each book in swirling gold letters.

"We thought you might like to collect autographs from your favourite festival acts," explained Lexy as Serena handed the blue book to Kirsty and the pink one to Rachel.

"Thank you!" Rachel gasped, her eyes shining.

"You'll sign our books, won't you," Kirsty asked eagerly, "Because you're our *very* favourite act!"

"We already have!" Serena replied, smiling. "Take a look."

Quickly Rachel and Kirsty flipped open their books. The Angels had signed the first pages of each, and they'd also added the first few lines of their hit song, *Key to My Heart*. Together the two girls began to read the words aloud, and The Angels sang along:

"When I'm with you I feel so glad,
The truest friend I ever had,
I know we two will never part,
And that's the real key to my heart!"

But The Angels' voices sounded hoarse
and croaky and out of tune. Lexy, Emilia
and Serena looked at each other
in dismay as they struggled to hit the
right notes.

"That was awful!"
Lexy fretted.

"Well, we *did*
perform the
opening concert
this morning,"
Serena pointed
out. "Maybe we
strained our voices
a bit."

"Yes, that must be it," Emilia agreed. Rachel and Kirsty didn't say anything, but they exchanged a secret, worried glance. They both knew *exactly* why The Angels' voices were so off-key...

When Kirsty and Rachel had arrived at Rainspell Island earlier that day, they'd had a wonderful surprise. Their old friend, Destiny the Pop Star Fairy, had arrived to invite them to watch the rehearsals for the Fairyland Music Festival. Destiny had whisked the girls off to Fairyland to meet the seven Pop Star Fairies whose magic helped her make sure that pop music everywhere was fun and tuneful.

But at the rehearsal the Pop Star Fairies hadn't been able to perform properly because sneaky Jack Frost and his goblins had stolen their seven magical musical clefs. Jack Frost had arrogantly declared that he was going to use the amazing powers of the magical clefs to become the biggest pop star in the world! Then he and his goblins had vanished in a flash of icy magic to Rainspell Island.

Rachel and Kirsty had agreed to help the fairies retrieve the magical clefs, knowing that pop music in both the human and the fairy worlds would never be the same again if they didn't find them all.

"Maybe we should rest and let our voices recover," Lexy suggested.

"That's a good idea," replied Serena.

"We'll pack the picnic things away,"
Kirsty offered.

"Thanks, girls," said Emilia. "Listen,
did you know that the band A-OK
are performing later? Well, the boys
are friends of ours and I'm sure they'd
love to sign your
autograph books."

"Great!"
Rachel
exclaimed.
"Kirsty and I
love A-OK."

"Why don't
you go along to
their rehearsal tent?"
Serena suggested. "You'll be able to get
in with those backstage passes we gave
you."

19

"We'll see you at the A-OK concert later, girls," said Lexy, and The Angels set off down the hill.

"The rest of the festival will be ruined if we don't find the missing clefs," Kirsty said with a frown as she and Rachel began collecting the empty plates.

"At least we managed to find Jessie the Lyrics Fairy's clef this morning," Rachel said. "That means the pop stars won't muddle up their lyrics any more."

"It was lucky Jessie's musical clef had *just* enough magic to make The Angels' concert a success, wasn't it?" said Kirsty. "But we need to find *all* the clefs to make *everything* right again."

"Which means we've got to keep a careful look-out for goblins at all times," Rachel replied.

Jack Frost had stolen the seven clefs from the Pop Star Fairies, and given some of them to his goblins to hide.

Kirsty reached for the picnic hamper to pack everything away. But suddenly there was a whooshing sound as a burst of dazzling fairy sparkles shot out of the hamper.

"Kirsty!" Rachel cried as she spotted a tiny figure dancing through the glittering mist. "It's Adele the Singing Coach Fairy!"

Jax Tempo in a Temper!

Adele greeted the girls with a wave of
her hand. She wore a deep pink tunic
over a floaty violet-coloured blouse with
white spots, and sparkly pink ballerina
flats on her feet. Her shiny hair was
chestnut-brown and drawn into a
neat bun.

"Hello, girls," Adele called, zooming towards them. "I'm so glad you enjoyed your picnic, but I heard The Angels trying to sing along with you. *All* the pop stars at the festival will be singing off-key like that if I don't find my magical musical clef – and fast!"

"We haven't seen Jack Frost yet, Adele," Kirsty told her. "But he must be here *somewhere*."

"Maybe he's hiding because he knows we're after him," Rachel said.

"I just *know* my magical musical clef is close by," Adele murmured wistfully. "Will you help me look for it, girls?"

Rachel and Kirsty nodded.

"We were about to go and watch A-OK rehearse," Kirsty explained. "We'll keep an eye out for goblins."

"Perfect!" Adele announced. "We can walk through the festival grounds and look for Jack Frost at the same time. But first I *must* tidy up for you before we go."

With one flick of Adele's wand, the plates, bowls, glasses and picnic rug rose up into the air and packed themselves neatly inside the hamper.

"I'd better hide as there are so many people around," Adele decided. Rachel opened her backpack and the little fairy flew inside, perching on top of Rachel's autograph book.

"Let's go, girls!" Adele called.

Rachel and Kirsty each took one handle of the picnic hamper and set off down the hill. Star Village was packed with people eager to try out the karaoke tent, the dance classes and all the other activities on offer, but the girls hurried through the crowds towards the backstage area where the rehearsal tents and the pop stars' trailers were situated.

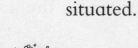

The girls dropped the picnic basket off at The Angels' silver trailer. Then they began to walk through the backstage area, searching for any sign of Jack Frost or his goblins. Suddenly Kirsty heard someone singing a familiar song:

I'm no fool
It's the number one rule,
I'm super-cool!

"Oh, we heard that rap song this morning in the karaoke tent!" Kirsty exclaimed, stopping to listen. "It's that new rapper, Jax Tempo."

"It sounds great!" Rachel said admiringly. "But where's it coming from?"

Kirsty pointed to an ice-blue trailer nearby. "Look, that trailer has *Jax Tempo* written on the door," she replied.

27

Rachel and Kirsty
followed the sound
of the music over
to the trailer.

"Jax Tempo
must be inside,"
whispered Kirsty.

"Do you think he'd be annoyed if we
asked for his autograph?" Rachel asked.

Kirsty shook her head. But before she
or Rachel could knock on the door,
the rapping inside the trailer stopped
abruptly.

"No, no, NO!" Jax Tempo yelled
angrily. Rachel and Kirsty recognised
his voice from earlier that day. "You
lot are supposed to do the background
harmonies – you're not supposed to join
in with my rap! Gobby, do you hear me?

Stop trying to take over my song!"

Dismayed, Rachel and Kirsty glanced at each other.

"Jax Tempo's really cross," Kirsty whispered.

"We'd better not bother him if he's in such a bad mood!" Rachel murmured. "Let's go, Kirsty."

The girls turned to leave. But as they did so the door of the trailer was suddenly flung open with a crash!

A-OK are not OK!

Rachel and Kirsty looked around curiously and saw a boy stomp out of Jax's trailer. The boy wore a bright green hoodie and a matching baseball cap pulled down low, hiding his face.

"I'm going to join a different band and then Jax Tempo will be sorry!" the boy muttered sulkily. "All he does is grumble and complain about my singing. He just doesn't realise how talented I am!"

"That must be Gobby," Rachel whispered as she and Kirsty walked past him.

Kirsty nodded. "Look, Rachel, there's the A-OK rehearsal tent," she said, spotting it ahead of them.

She and Kirsty stopped to find their backstage passes. As Rachel took hers out of her backpack, Adele smiled and waved.

"We're keeping our eyes open for your magical musical clef!" Rachel whispered to her.

The girls hurried over to A-OK's rehearsal tent and showed their passes to the security guard outside.

As they went in,
Kirsty thought
she heard
the sound
of scurrying
footsteps close
behind them.
She glanced
around but couldn't
see anyone.

"That's funny," Rachel said a few
seconds later, as they made their way
into the main part of the tent, "I thought
I felt something brush against me, but I
must have imagined it because there's no
one here except you and me."

"And A-OK, of course!" Kirsty
whispered. "Look, there they are,
standing near that piano!"

The four members of A-OK – Jez,
Amir, Rio and Finn – were grouped in
front of the piano. Rachel and Kirsty
stopped shyly a
little distance
away and
gazed
at the
familiar
faces
of the
boys with
delight.
There was
also an older
man with black hair
and dark, flashing eyes seated on the
piano stool. As the girls watched, the
man shook his head in despair.

"That was *terrible!*" the man announced dramatically. "Again, please." He played an introduction and the four boys cleared their throats, then began to sing.

I'd climb the highest mountain,
Just to be with you,
I'd swim the deepest river,
Just to be with you...

Rachel and
Kirsty
recognised
the song
as one
of A-OK's
biggest hits, but just
like The Angels, the boys' voices
sounded harsh and off-key. Looking
furious, the man stopped playing.

"That was even worse!" he announced. "You sound more like a bunch of farm animals than a pop group. People will blame *me* if they hear such a horrible noise. Me, Alto Adams, the best singing coach in the world! Now…" He stood up from the piano and glared at the boys. "Listen to this note and sing it after me."

Alto Adams took a breath and then tried to sing one note. But like the boys, his own voice was croaky and completely out of tune. Alto looked horrified.

"What's happening?" he groaned. Sinking down into his seat again, he pounded on the piano keys in frustration. "The concert is starting soon. What are we going to do?"

The members of A-OK glanced at each other in despair, but said nothing. As the girls quietly took their autograph books out of their backpacks, Rachel could see that Adele was looking very miserable.

"No pop stars here or in Fairyland will be able to sing beautifully again until I find my magical clef!" Adele whispered sadly.

Just then Rio looked their way and saw Rachel and Kirsty waiting patiently nearby, autograph books in hand.

"Sorry you had to listen to that, girls," Rio said, shrugging his shoulders apologetically. "We're not usually this bad, are we, guys?"

The others shook their heads.

"Nothing's going right today, for some reason," Jez sighed. "Even Alto's having problems."

They all glanced over at Alto who was sitting gloomily on the piano stool.

"I hope we're not interrupting your rehearsal," Kirsty said.

"No way!" Finn replied. "We're glad to take a break."

"Do you think we could have your autographs?" asked Rachel.

"Are you sure you still want them after hearing us sing?" Amir joked, but Rachel and Kirsty could see that he looked just as anxious as the others.

Jez, Amir, Rio and Finn gathered around and signed the girls' autograph books one by one. They handed the books back to Rachel and Kirsty who thanked them, looking very pleased.

And, then right at that moment, something magical happened. A clear, beautiful voice came out of nowhere, filling the tent with its pure, melodious singing:

"I'd climb the highest mountain,
Just to be with you,
I'd swim the deepest river,
Just to be with you..."

Alto Adams leapt up from the piano stool. "Who's that?" he demanded. "Come out and show yourself!"

Rachel and Kirsty could hardly believe their eyes when Gobby crawled out from behind the piano.

"Gobby must have sneaked past the security guard when we came in," Rachel murmured to Kirsty. "So we *weren't* imagining things!"

A-OK were staring at Gobby in amazement, too. Excitedly Alto rushed over and slapped him on the back. "Congratulations, my friend, your singing is wonderful!" Alto exclaimed. "In fact, it's A-OK!" And he beamed at Gobby.

Confused, Rachel turned to Kirsty. "I don't get it!" Rachel murmured. "How can Gobby sing so well when Adele's clef is missing?"

The A-OK boys had gone over to congratulate Gobby on his singing, too.

Gobby puffed out his chest, looking very pleased with himself.

"So can I join the band?" he asked Alto eagerly.

"Of course," Alto agreed, shaking Gobby's hand. "We'd be honoured to have you."

"Hurrah!" Gobby yelled, jumping up and down with glee. As he did so, Kirsty noticed a necklace fly out from under the top of his hoodie.

Then Kirsty's heart began to pound with excitement – she could see that the charm on the necklace was Adele's missing magical clef!

"Gobby's a goblin, and he's got Adele's clef!" Kirsty whispered, pointing the necklace out to Rachel. "*That's* why he can sing so well."

"No wonder poor Jax Tempo was in such a bad mood," Rachel remembered. "Gobby was probably up to all sorts of mischief in his trailer! But how are we going to get the magical clef back from Gobby without anyone seeing?"

Gobby the Star!

Frowning, Rachel and Kirsty stared at each other, wondering what to do.

"Stand next to the piano while I play, and sing the song right through," Alto told Gobby.

"All right," Gobby agreed. "Can I have a brand-new outfit for the show this afternoon?"

"With a voice like that, you can wear whatever you like!" Alto told him.

As Gobby began to sing, Rachel drew Kirsty aside a little.

"What Gobby just said has given me an idea," Rachel whispered. "But we need to get out of here quickly because we're going to need Adele's magic to help us."

Quietly the girls slipped out of the tent and then hurried around to the back of it, out of everyone's sight. There Rachel opened her backpack and Adele fluttered out.

"I heard everything you said, girls," Adele cried.

"Gobby the goblin has my clef, and that's why he has such an amazing singing voice!"

"I have an idea about how to get your clef back, Adele," Rachel told her. "Can you change Kirsty and me into fairies?"

"No sooner said than done!" Adele replied. One wave of her wand, and a puff of rainbow-coloured fairy dust transformed the girls into fairies with the same thin gossamer wings as Adele.

47

"We must find A-OK's trailer," Rachel said, as the girls whizzed up into the air.

"It's probably quite close to the rehearsal tent," Kirsty suggested. Quickly the three of them zoomed higher into the sky so that they wouldn't be spotted by the people below, and then they began circling the backstage area. Very soon they spotted a large gold trailer with A-OK written in black glitter on the door.

Adele pointed her wand at the door and a stream of fairy sparkles unlocked it, opening it just a crack so that Adele and the girls could slip inside.

The trailer was very long with a bathroom and a lounge at one end. At the other end each A-OK member had his own dressing area. In each one there was a large mirror surrounded by lights and a glittery sign with the band member's name on it Their stage costumes were hanging on hooks.

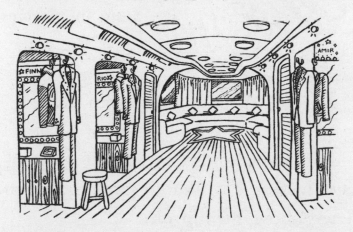

"Gobby will want his *own* dressing area," Rachel said with a grin. "Adele, could you make one for him?"

Adele nodded. There was a space
between Finn and Rio's area with piles
of spare clothes stacked
in it. Adele waved
her wand briskly
and the clothes
whisked up
into the air and
hung themselves
out of the way
on hangers on
an empty clothes
rail. More of Adele's
magic created a dressing-area for Gobby
with his name written in sparkling green
letters above the mirror.

"Gobby needs a stage costume," said
Rachel. "I suppose it'll have to be green
or he won't like it! Any ideas, Kirsty?"

"How about some green trainers with flashes of white on the sides?" suggested Kirsty.

Adele nodded and conjured up a pair of emerald-green trainers with dazzling white flashes.

"Maybe he'd like some dark green jeans," said Rachel. "Oh, and a belt with a gold G-shaped buckle?"

Adele flicked her wand and the jeans and belt joined the trainers in Gobby's dressing-area. The girls then added a green and purple hoodie and a matching baseball cap.

"And now for the most important thing of all," said Rachel. "Adele, we need a clef necklace, exactly like yours."

"But without the magical powers, obviously!" Adele said, her eyes twinkling. A mist of fairy glitter swirled briefly around in the air, and then the necklace appeared, hanging on one of the hooks.

Rachel smiled. "All we need now is Gobby himself!" she declared. "Let's go and find him."

Quickly the three friends flew out of the trailer, Adele locking the door again with her magic. They headed for the A-OK rehearsal tent, but on the way there they heard shouts and cheers coming from over by the stages.

"What's that noise?" asked Rachel,

stopping and hovering in mid air.

"Look at that little stage over there," Kirsty said. "There's a crowd of fans around the A-OK boys – and Gobby's with them!"

Keeping high up in the air so that no one could see them, Adele, Rachel and Kirsty flew over to the stage. It was surrounded by life-size cut-outs of the four boys, posters of the band and stalls selling A-OK T-shirts, CDs and programmes. Rio, Finn, Jez and Amir were signing autographs and chatting to the fans who were crowding around the stage, and so was Gobby! Rachel, Adele and Kirsty could see that the goblin was enjoying every moment, posing for photos and scribbling his name in autograph books.

"Gobby, it's great that you've joined A-OK!" called a girl from the crowd. "But are you feeling nervous about the concert later? You look a bit green!"

"Er – I'm so excited about being in A-OK, I feel sick!" Gobby replied. "But I'm sure I'll be all right when I get onstage later."

"Can the band sing something for us right now?" another fan shouted eagerly. There were cheers of delight at this suggestion.

"You'll have to wait for the concert, folks," Alto told the crowd of fans. "The boys need to rest their voices now."

The fans looked disappointed, but they continued clamouring for autographs, shouting questions at the band and snapping pictures with their mobile phones. They all wanted photos of the band's newest member, Gobby.

"Gobby's loving all the attention!" Adele whispered to Kirsty and Rachel. "How on earth are we going to get him away from all his new fans?"

"I have an idea!" replied Kirsty. "Listen, this is what we'll do…"

Kirsty's Clever Plan

Adele, Rachel and Kirsty flew to hide behind one of the T-shirt stalls. There, out of sight, Adele's magic returned the girls to their human size once more. Then Adele hid herself in Rachel's backpack, and the two girls hurried out to join the crowd of fans around A-OK.

"Hello, Gobby!" Kirsty called, smiling up at him. "We saw you earlier today, remember?"

"We didn't realise you were such a big star!" Rachel added. She waved her autograph book in the air. "Please can we have your autograph?"

"Of course!" Gobby agreed graciously, holding out his hand. "And please will you sing something for us?" Kirsty added, giving him her autograph book. Gobby shot an anxious glance at Alto Adams on the other side of the stage.

"I'm not supposed to sing anything until the concert," he muttered as he scrawled his name in the book.

"Oh, *please*," Rachel pleaded.

"You have such a wonderful voice!"
Kirsty added. Looking very pleased with
himself, Gobby cleared his throat and
sang softly:

"I'd climb the highest mountain,
Just to be with you,
I'd swim the deepest river,
Just to be with you…"

But Gobby didn't look *quite* so pleased
when Rachel and Kirsty instantly
clapped their hands
over their ears. The
girls had horrified
expressions on
their faces.

"Is there something
wrong with your
voice, Gobby?" asked
Rachel with a frown.

Gobby stared at her in disbelief. "No!" he snapped. "Why?"

"Because you sound awful!" Kirsty told him. It wasn't true at all. Gobby's voice still beautiful, but Kirsty had a plan.

"No, I don't!" Gobby gasped. He fumbled at the neck of his hoodie, feeling

for the magical clef as if to make sure it was still there. "My singing's *amazing*!" Rachel and Kirsty shrugged and glanced at each other.

"Maybe you're just feeling a bit nervous about the concert this afternoon," Kirsty suggested.

"Yes, you need to relax a little," Rachel added. "I bet you've got a fabulous stage outfit all ready for you in the A-OK trailer. That'll make you feel like a real star!"

Gobby cheered up instantly and nodded. "Yes, maybe I should go and check it out," he said thoughtfully.

"We'll come with you," said Kirsty, winking at Rachel. "We saw the trailer earlier on."

Gobby slipped off the stage and hurried away without Alto Adams or the other boys noticing. The girls went with him, leading the way to the trailer. Then Rachel and Kirsty saw a very faint cloud of shimmering fairy dust as Adele peeped out of Rachel's backpack and used her magic to unlock the door again.

"Oh!" Gobby gasped with delight as he climbed into the trailer and saw the dressing areas. "Look, it says *Gobby* over there on that glittery sign!"

"That's your new outfit hanging on those hooks," Kirsty said, pointing at the clothes.

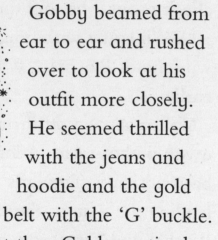

Gobby beamed from ear to ear and rushed over to look at his outfit more closely. He seemed thrilled with the jeans and hoodie and the gold belt with the 'G' buckle.

But then Gobby noticed the copy of the clef necklace hanging on one of the hooks. Rachel and Kirsty saw him frown and begin to sing softly:

I'd climb the highest mountain,
Just to be with you,
I'd swim the deepest river,
Just to be with you…

Gobby seemed to be checking that the magic of the clef necklace he was wearing was still working. Immediately Rachel and Kirsty groaned loudly and shook their heads in despair.

"What's the matter?" Gobby demanded angrily.

"Your voice sounds awful, Gobby!" Rachel exclaimed. "I hate to tell you this, but your singing is really bad!"

Just Like Magic!

Gobby looked very angry. Meanwhile Kirsty picked up the fake necklace and slipped it over her head.

"That necklace makes you look like a star, Kirsty!" Rachel exclaimed admiringly. "Why don't you trying singing a pop song?"

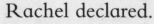

"OK!" Kirsty said with a grin, and she began to sing:

"*When I'm with you I feel so glad,*
The truest friend I ever had,
I know we two will never part,
And that's the real key to my heart!"

Kirsty knew she sounded terrible, but Rachel cheered and clapped loudly.

"I never realised you had such a great singing voice, Kirsty!" Rachel declared.

Gobby was now looking very confused.

"I think the other goblins have been playing a trick on me," he murmured to himself.

Then he pointed at Kirsty. "I want
THAT necklace!" Gobby announced.
"This one I'm wearing doesn't work
any more!"

"Are you sure, Gobby?" Kirsty asked
innocently.

"Yes, I'm sure!" Gobby
snapped. He pulled
off Adele's necklace
and threw it
impatiently to the
floor. Instantly
Adele zoomed
out of Rachel's
backpack.
Swooping down, she
caught the necklace
before it hit the ground and immediately
it shrank to its fairy-size.

Gobby gave a shout of rage. "It's a fairy trick!" he yelled, and stamped his foot. Sulkily he barged out of the trailer, nearly knocking over the A-OK boys as they came through the door. Jez, Amir, Finn and Rio looked very surprised. Quickly Adele flew to hide once more inside Rachel's backpack, clutching her magical musical clef and beaming happily.

"What's the matter with Gobby?" asked Amir.

"He brought us here to see his stage outfit," Kirsty replied. "But it looks like he's changed his mind and he doesn't want to be in the band after all!"

"That's a shame," said Finn. "But we were practising our songs on the way over here, and as we reached the trailer, our singing voices came back!"

"It was just like magic!" Jez added, and Rachel and Kirsty laughed. The A-OK boys had no idea just how right they were!

The concert took place later that afternoon. Rachel and Kirsty were lucky enough to get places right at the front of the stage, and they danced and sang along to all of A-OK's songs with the rest of the crowd of festival-goers. Adele joined in too, still hidden inside Rachel's backpack, and because she was nearby, there was just enough magic around to ensure that the concert was a success.

As A-OK finished off with one of their
well-known hit songs, accompanied by
a spectacular dance routine, Rachel and
Kirsty clapped until their hands were sore
and cheered until they were hoarse.

The A-OK boys took a bow and
then bounced off the stage. Quickly
Rachel and Kirsty moved away from the
crowds, and then Adele popped up out of
Rachel's backpack.

"Wasn't it a great
concert, Adele?"
asked Rachel with
a grin. "Thanks to
your magic!"

Adele smiled,
too, touching
the clef that hung
around her neck.

71

"It was wonderful," she replied. "But we must find *all* the magical musical clefs to bring harmony again to pop stars *everywhere!*"

"We'll keep looking, Adele," Kirsty assured her.

"Thank you!" Adele called. Then, with a flick of her wand, she was whisked off to Fairyland.

"Five more magical clefs to go!"
Rachel remarked, as she and Kirsty
made their way back to the Walkers'
tent.
"Do you think we'll find another one
today, Kirsty?"
"I hope so!" Kirsty replied.

Now Kirsty and Rachel
must help...

Vanessa the Dance Steps Fairy

Read on for a sneak peek...

"Hooray!" cheered Rachel Walker, as she and her best friend Kirsty Tate walked onto Rainspell Beach. "The sun is shining, we're on holiday together *and* we're at the Rainspell Island Music Festival."

"It's been wonderful so far, hasn't it?" Kirsty agreed with a smile.

It was certainly turning out to be a day the girls would never forget. First, they'd seen their favourite band The Angels open the show. Next to perform were the boy band, A-OK, who had wowed the crowd with their melodic harmonies. And best of all, Kirsty and Rachel had found themselves caught up in an exciting new fairy adventure, this time with the Pop Star Fairies!

"Hi, girls," came three familiar voices just then.

Rachel and Kirsty turned to see Lexy, Serena and Emilia – also known as The Angels.

"Hi," beamed Kirsty. She and Rachel had met the band before when they'd helped Destiny the Pop Star Fairy, and were lucky enough to have backstage passes to the festival. Being friends with pop stars was almost as much fun as being friends with the fairies!

"Did you see A-OK? Weren't they fab?" said Lexy.

"I didn't know they were such great performers," said Emilia, kicking off her sandals and wiggling her bare toes in the golden sand. "Those boys rocked!"

"I can't wait to see Sasha Sharp tonight," Rachel put in. "She's a brilliant dancer."

"Sasha's amazing," Serena agreed. "Have you seen the video to her new song, *Let's Dance*? She does such a cool routine. How does it go again?"

The Angels started singing Sasha's latest hit, and they all tried to remember the dance moves...

Read Vanessa the Dance Steps Fairy to find out what adventures are in store for Kirsty and Rachel!